The Urbana Free Library

To renew: call 217-367-4057
or go to **urbanafreelibrary.org**
and select **My Account**

THE PARTHENON BOMBER

THE
PARTHENON
BOMBER

Christos Chrissopoulos
TRANSLATED BY JOHN CULLEN

 Other Press New York

Original title: Ο βομβιστής του Παρθενώνα by Christos Chrissopoulos

Copyright © 2010 by Christos Chrissopoulos / Kastaniotis Editions, Athens
In accordance with Iris Literary Agency, irislit@otenet.gr

English translation copyright © 2017 by Other Press

Epigraph on page 69 translated from the Italian by Jeff Fort
(Brooklyn, NY: Zone Books, 2007)

Production editor: Yvonne E. Cárdenas
Text designer: Julie Fry
This book was set in Whitman with Interstate.

10 9 8 7 6 5 4 3 2 1

Library of Congress Cataloging-in-Publication Data
Names: Chrissopoulos, Christos, 1968– author. | Cullen, John, 1942– translator.
Title: The Parthenon bomber / by Christos Chrissopoulos ;
    translated by John Cullen.
Other titles: Ο βομβιστής του Παρθενώνα. English
Description: New York : Other Press, 2017.
Identifiers: LCCN 2016052902 (print) | LCCN 2017010146 (ebook) |
    ISBN 9781590518366 (hardback) | ISBN 9781590518373 (e-book)
Subjects: LCSH: Parthenon (Athens, Greece) — Fiction. | Terrorism — Fiction. |
    Cultural property — Destruction and pillage — Greece — Fiction. |
    BISAC: FICTION / Cultural Heritage. | FICTION / Alternative History. |
    FICTION / Literary.
Classification: LCC PA5614.H77 B6613 2017 (print) | LCC PA5614.H77 (ebook) |
    DDC 889.3/4 — dc23
LC record available at https://lccn.loc.gov/2016052902

Earth's crazy daydreamers are we,
with blazing hearts and furious eyes:
the unredeemed thinkers, the tragic lovers.
A thousand suns course through our blood
and the vision of infinity pursues us from all sides.
Form cannot master us.
We have fallen in love with the essence of our existence
and in all our loves that very essence is what we adore.
We are the great zealots and the great deniers.
Within us we contain the cosmos, and without it we are nothing.
Our days are a fire and our nights a sea.
Human laughter echoes around us.

We are the heralds of chaos.

—Yorgos Makris, "We few…" (1950)[1]

1 A PROBABLE MONOLOGUE
SPOKEN BY THE PERPETRATOR, CH.K.

The only sounds are those of furniture being moved. Chairs scraping across the floor. Then footsteps. The pressing of buttons on some electronic device. Finally, the sound of someone breathing heavily, close to the microphone. A pause of several seconds. Absolute silence.

When I first started, I didn't have the least notion of how I ought to go about it. I had no plan. I had no particular ideal. What set things in motion was an impulse, a kind of inner surge that brought me here. It might just as well have carried me anywhere.

There wasn't any first day. There was no definite beginning. I can't identify any certain inspiration, nor did I deliberately pursue any specific goal. The first things I considered — or rather the first things I clearly, vividly imagined — were the consequences of the act. That's all. The reverberations of the act on the front pages of the newspapers, in the first words of the radio announcers, in the first pictures on the TV news. The consequences . . . The act, looming above the city, sending shock waves over the neighborhoods and the avenues. Hanging down from the city's ceiling. Nailed to the clouds. The act, now become news. The act, on everyone's lips. The act, present everywhere, all the time. The act, which was now our common property. The pleasure of secretly recognizing it as my own.

That was the first stage. Today I can say so with certainty. The first thing that fascinated me was the notion that everyone would talk about what I'd done, everyone would be aware of it and completely stunned by it, but no one except me would be able to delight in it. I alone would have anticipated it, and every time someone talked about it, every time I read an account of it, everything, the least detail, would contribute to making it more deliciously real. And this particular act would be utterly mine, mine and mine alone.

In our city, it's difficult to believe that any single thing really belongs to you. Your successes are shared between you and those who annex them for themselves. As for failures, nobody owns them because they're so rarely admitted. And so there's nothing you can own without sharing it. Except, perhaps, an utter delusion: an act committed with full consciousness.

I greatly feared that my act would be misinterpreted. On many occasions, that fear made me back off and postpone the execution of my plan. I didn't want to be stigmatized as one more heinous criminal. A charming lunatic. A madman. A convenient stereotype.

Our city possesses one single, distinctive monument. An emblem that fulfills many functions, precisely because It's unique. There's no other identifiable landmark in the vicinity, and were we to lose that unique proof of our origins, that emblematic place we all believe belongs to us by right, then we would feel as though we were living in a foreign country. We'd feel artificial. Part of a board game, perhaps, or at the bottom of an aquarium.

The lights in our city are colored. Yellow or orange. Our city's slow, but she gets impatient sometimes, just as we all do. Sometimes she knows where she's going, sometimes she stumbles around. We and our city are the same. Wherever we go, we carry her in our pockets. And should we get tired, we put her down, wherever we may be, and enter her. We curl up and live enclosed in her entrails. Inside the hot, arid city, we're always singing the same songs to ourselves. In a low voice. Over and over.

It's very important to be clear about one's motives. I had no intention of doing harm. I had no intention of doing harm. I didn't want to destroy. Destruction wasn't my goal. There aren't any rational explanations for it. There's only the illusion of autonomous action; only action has meaning. I don't represent anything. It simply belongs to me, that's all. This act belongs to me.

He seems to hesitate a little and lose his train of thought. Then he starts thinking out loud, as though talking to himself.

In our city, all citizens have the right to follow their own paths — or should I say each has the right to follow *his* own path? Every time I cross a street, I do it from the same spot. I go up and down the stairs. Thirteen steps per floor. Four on the sidewalk. Two every time I get on the bus.

Another two when I get off. Four steps on the opposite sidewalk, twenty to the door. Everything here seems to be a stride or two away. The neighborhoods touch hands, making an uninterrupted chain of houses that all seem to be leaning on one another. One street passes the baton to the next, and the only thing that changes is the name. There's nothing very unusual in this continuity. It doesn't surprise me at all. This isn't the only place where it occurs. It's just that here nothing's farther away than a single breath. And so everyone who lives here has the impression that you can take a short walk and see the whole city. And the horizon disappears behind the buildings so often that you think visiting every corner of this little world would be easy, requiring no more effort than going out the door and circling the block.

But it's not only space that can be measured in paces here. Time too gives you the illusion that you could cross it easily, in a single longish step. There's nothing very unusual in this impression. It doesn't surprise me at all. This isn't the only place where it occurs. If only there weren't this merciless sun. The dust swirling around you is so thick you could hold it in your hand. If there weren't this heat...it makes taking even one step so difficult. Everything here imprisons you in light.

He goes on slowly, as if trying to remember something buried in the past.

Everything began with an observation: The symbol of our city occupies her highest point. It stands there, erect and central, and we light It up so that It never escapes our sight, not even for a moment. Our city's symbol has a name, but we refer to It as a depersonalized entity. We say, "Look at *It*," or "I saw *It*," or "near *It*," or "under *Its* shadow," and so forth.

Even as a small child, I would watch It reigning over our world from up there. I'd hear everybody extol Its beauty and say how light and harmonious It was. How magisterially It accorded with the landscape and transcended human dimensions. Everyone declares It a masterpiece. It symbolizes all that is lofty and beautiful. Who made It? That's not important anymore. It exists, and that's enough. People here don't appreciate the value of what we have. In this city, nothing belongs to us, ownership doesn't exist here. As for pride in having It among us, we don't even own that sentiment. We borrow it from others.

Many a time have I gone up there to see It close, to study It. It's something we never get used to. When we go up and get close to It, we give It a few furtive glances and then we turn our eyes to the city lying down there at our feet, and that puts us into a bad mood, because she's unworthy of It, and no matter what we do, we will never become worthy of such a masterpiece.

Many a time have I climbed the steps leading to It. I'd act as if I knew nothing about It, I'd forget all the praise that's been heaped upon It, and I'd put It to the test. I'd say, "Well, here I am. Overcome me. We're alone here, you and me. Captivate me with that charm of yours." It couldn't do it. I saw It again and again. In all seasons, at all hours. I saw the sun spring up inside It. I saw It sullen, covered with clouds, and lit by the floodlights, which haloed It in orange light. I gave It every chance It asked for. And yet, It failed.

What happened with It is what often happens with our cherished ideals. People around you never stop pointing out how perfect It is, everyone vies with one another to repeat that It has no flaw, everybody adores It. You don't understand. You ask for explanations, and you're treated to the same hackneyed phrases. Doubt does not exist. In the end, you're a believer too. Even if you're still a little hesitant, sooner or later you add your voice to the choir of praise. Because it's hard to express a dissenting opinion when everyone else is in agreement, and if they all sing praises of Its excellence, in the end you join the choir, because you can't stand being ranked with the philistines, the foolish, or the reactionaries. So then you too set about perpetuating the fairy tale, and not only do you end up believing it, you also become its passionate defender. Like all of us.

An attentive look at our city suffices. The homes, the neighborhoods, ourselves. The gob of spit on the street. The stink of a sweating body. The bad language. The dry air. The city. Our land: a few square meters for each of us.

Some people love It because It's simple, light, pure, chaste. But where are these elements, this simplicity and lightness and purity and nobility, in their own lives? If beauty isn't a value they respect, how can they love It because It's beautiful? Why don't they look for beauty in themselves, in their immediate surroundings? Why are they incapable of understanding beauty? Why doesn't it interest them or touch them?

In our city, beauty has long since disappeared under the orange lights that permanently illuminate the streets. Beauty is sophistication and obsequiousness. Beauty is absent. It's a forgotten virtue. In our city, pride is nonexistent. We're all living on borrowed greatness. Many would agree, but they're cowards and won't admit it. So that was my starting point: It's not as perfect as people think. And then I realized I had nothing left, because I'd given back even the little I'd borrowed.

He stops abruptly, then continues.

Even though our city doesn't have very clear borders, everything follows a strict arrangement, not just spatial but also temporal. Life is clearly divided into pairs: here/there, ahead/behind, right/left, east/west, before/after. Pairs that set up an indisputable, vertical boundary every time they're used. An opposition that splits the city like a knife slash. Sometimes it's an obstacle that creates a split in the landscape: here/there. At other times, it's the surprise caused by an unexpected change: before/after. For certain people, it's the intolerable cruelty of a historic past: then/now.

So every time, you have to take a side. Except that, here again, it's doubly deceptive. On the one hand, geography seems to defy its own rules: a sidewalk that splits down the middle, empty squares bounded exclusively by general desolation, streets continually renamed while others retain their rather outdated historic designations, complete with the attendant nostalgia. The feeling of a perpetual worksite: excavated avenues, buildings whose use is subject to sudden change, others whose mysterious future purposes you can't possibly imagine. And then there's something else besides, an additional suspicion that envelops everybody who walks down those streets. Everything here is, at one and the same moment, both past and present. Here, history takes the form of a triple denial, an indifference that the city herself seems to repeat again and again: I don't remember — it doesn't concern me — I don't know.

He hesitates a moment and then goes on, but now it's as though he's reading from some text.

I went back to see It again. It hadn't changed. It was, as before, bathed in orange light. This confirmation increased my feelings of uneasiness, because an iniquity, an absurdity was all too apparent. The way It hulked there, ruling over all. It was a more powerful adversary than I had envisioned. It didn't collapse on me in a heap at the first blow. I had been naïve to think of It as just standing there, simply overrated, up on the summit of the city. No. Its strength resided elsewhere. Its power was something different. Sometime later, I went up to Its base once again. I stood right in front of It for a few minutes, and then I sat on a stone and stared up at It fearlessly.

This time It looked naked, defenseless. Patched on every side. Supported by splints of some sort, made of metal beams and lumber. With crutches to keep It upright. Entire bits of It missing. It was weak, bent, bony.

We're constantly maintaining It. Technicians never leave It alone. Experts don't take their eyes off It for a second. We will not allow It to collapse.

I went away perplexed and returned the next day, ready to confront It. My resolve was firm. Because the better you understand something, the fitter you are to take it on. Whereas with something that's a mystery to you, you'll have trouble finding its weak point.

It was standing there in front of me again, and I could feel Its power. I saw how people — including me — approached It. Slowly, cautiously, engrossed in devotion. As though prostrating themselves. They were circling It with their cameras and photographing It with the joy you feel at capturing the aura of some indomitable grandeur. They were acknowledging Its possession of a mysterious force. Which, in fact, It had. I will concede that sincerely. It was mighty.

That day I went away again, again having accomplished nothing. Overwhelmed by the mere sight of It. I went down the steps, leaving It behind me, and the city lights looked almost charming. I felt Its presence weighing on my shoulders, and the floodlights' orange illumination was so strong that it bathed the roofs of the surrounding houses in gold. Then, all of a sudden, It revealed Itself to me. I saw It printed on a small child's T-shirt. Farther on, Its name was on a street sign. In the inscription on some glass building. Written in Roman script on a cigarette lighter. Its image was on a piece of crumpled paper tossed onto the street. It appeared on all sides. It didn't belong to us at all, and yet we had stuck It up everywhere.

Our city is poor, and we are strange people. We want to be left alone. Our land seems to be encircled with distorting mirrors. Wherever we look, we behold bizarre images of ourselves. We've been that way here for years. Heirless by choice. With It as our symbol. I hereby declare that I want to understand just how this works. Its symbolism is always double. It always works on a system of opposites. Not only between private and public but also between the city and its residents, the exception and the rule, reigning and governing.

More certain now that I knew more, I again climbed the steps that shone from being so much trodden upon. I stood before It without speaking. This time It faced me with a fiery glow, wrapped in the orange mist of the floodlights. And It had as an ally the visitors' general unanimity: "Silence! It represents us! Leave It in peace!"

"Lies!" I yelled. "Lies! What is this thing you want to adopt as your own? Do you know It? Have you any idea what It is?"

What we don't know scares us. We take up a defensive position behind something familiar and lie low. We tenderly embrace what resembles us and we glower at what's different. And as long as those others remain far away from us, we content ourselves with glowering at them, in secret. Always hiddenly, discreetly, we're not barbarians...Always in secret, but keeping our fists tightly clenched in our pockets.

In this city, we live only among our own kind, and for a long time we've managed to scare off all foreigners. Visitors aren't needed anymore, and whoever arrives from far away remains isolated among us. And so, even in misfortune, we don't need anyone but ourselves. We avoid other people, and we don't want to hear talk about anything new. We need nothing more than what we already have. We know what's necessary; we reject innovations. If someone wants to separate himself from the rest of us, he becomes undesirable — our city doesn't forgive that kind of initiative. Such a person will be derided. He'll be stripped, and then afterward he'll put his old clothes back on.

Everybody here has the place that suits them. And our life is whatever we do in the public space. For the most part, such activities are unconscious and automatic: We stand up, we walk, we consume, we talk, we move about, we write. In the sequence of events from inertia through to movement and from obedience through to transgression, there are unconscious acts but also deliberate actions: We sing in the street, we write on a wall, we break an object, we stumble, we light a fire, we do theater, we run after each other, we swipe something, we hit, we pollute, we dance . . . In other words: We live outside, in the street, on an expanse of ground that we share with everyone else while we each remain alone. The street, then, becomes a familiar space — or rather an appropriated space — that's more or less equivalent to a private room. A space where we feel we have some rights. And in this way, every event becomes an act. It's something that "someone does." Life doesn't unfold "inside the city" anymore but "on the city itself," on top of the city, on her body. The city is no longer a container (we live inside the city and have our dreams there), she's a combination of object and game (we live in leading to our city's highest point. The ultimate refuge. Should doubt seize us, if only for an instant, should some disagreeable thought cross our mind, should the city herself be going through a difficult moment, should we be in need for any reason whatsoever, we must be able to climb up to It immediately, without problems and without delay. Because without It, there is no hope.

And so for the nth time, I climbed the wide, uphill road leading to It. Evening had fallen, and clouds of impatient insects were buzzing around the orange light. I sat down on the same rock and avoided looking It in the face, because I knew that at the first glance, It would collapse to the ground in a heap. In the end, I raised my head abruptly and stared straight at It. I saw It shudder in surprise. It shifted. It nearly stumbled before my eyes, but It didn't fall. I tried to imagine It collapsing, but I couldn't. I had insufficient imagination.

It was discredited, It was decrepit, but It didn't fall. I got up, feeling exhausted and nearly defeated. I descended the slippery steps, blind with chagrin. I went home and shut myself inside. And even so, within my walls, behind my closed shutters, up above the ceiling, penetrating the hard concrete, Its presence entered and surrounded me. Where did Its cells' vital center lie buried? Where was Its heart?

Our city has the strength to allow any type of incident, so that everything becomes possible within her territory — "This is a city where anything can happen" — and moreover everything can become possible anywhere in her territory: "This is a city where anything can happen everywhere." As a result, our urban geography is no longer characterized by specific, favorite spots — "places in the city where things happen" — but by an unprecedented dispersion of such spots to every corner of the city, from the most privileged to the most marginal: "In this city, all places seem to become one." Nevertheless, despite this ostensible freedom, my intended act was still inconceivable.

But that same evening, as I sat in my room with the shutter slats half open and the orange light from the street filtering through the curtains, everything was clarified, simply and quietly, as if my plan had matured long ago.

Here in our city, we're constantly invoking It; no moment passes without someone making some reference to It. You would think we were all living in Its past. We invoke It with wonderment when we feel paltry, something that happens often, or when we realize how poor we are. Invoking It suffices us. And that's how we make do, because we don't like thinking about anything. The only thing we really like is to say, "Look up there, look at the top of the city. Look at It!" We're not interested in anything else.

In this city of ours, nothing belongs to us anymore. Nothing new happens, and there are no surprises. There are no unexpected emotions. In this city, everything looks evanescent. And if we're asked about it, we whisper quietly among ourselves that things couldn't be better than they are. Because, we say, "Look up there. Look at the acme of the city." And we feel like dwarfs and giants, both at the same time. When we feel like dwarfs, we say that others fear us because It's up there at the top of the city. And when we feel gigantic, it's the same: We raise our eyes to It in expectation.

Here in this city of ours, you can't simply trust in your imagination. I lay down in the midst of my books and set about dreaming of the effects my act would have. I tried to imagine it, tried to imagine that it had become my property. Here in this city of ours, we all dream of having some property of our own. What would happen first? The surprise. The consequences.

No one can believe it. Everybody's whispering and terrified. No one wants to believe it. They all run to see it with their own eyes, to get confirmation. Did that really happen? They think their senses are playing tricks on them. They don't believe their eyes. Nothing is certain, nothing's definite yet. What's left? Only shattered rock. The flame-ravaged pedestal. A fine column of smoke, rising amid the twisted iron supports and lit by orange lights. Some floodlights are still working. It's late afternoon. Twilight. The hour when the color of the sky over the city turns a deep blue. The streetlights come on, one after another, and the air is refreshed with the exhalations of the earth. The magnificent canvas of the heavens comes to life and unfolds above the long, thin flames, interlaced like ribbons, to be almost instantly dispersed from the summit of the city, scattered in every direction, and lost. A light, ethereal veil spreads over the scene, with the firmament as background. And yet only a few seconds have passed.

And then will I be, for the first time in my life, the lord and master of my own unique act. Everyone else will be running around like lunatics, bent on rescuing what they think can be saved. Helicopters will circle the hill, and the streets will be slashed by red sirens, carving their way through the thick crowds. The hum of the city will swell, the trucks, the people, the sirens . . . And all those who aren't outside will remain glued to their screens, getting a helicopter's-eye view of the event, and they'll pray for something to happen, something that will turn back time.

Time, however, cannot be turned back, for suddenly everything is upside down. The present is expressed in the past tense; the past is no longer what it was. The future was the past. Ambition was recollection. Dreams were memories. And now, for the first time, we have no starting point, and perhaps for that reason we'll succeed in choosing a destination. The highways are closed, and the stories aren't worth anything anymore. Everything has been overthrown by an act no one but me can lay claim to. By an act that can't be circumscribed in any way. An act I own, an act that belongs to me. The smashing of the symbol.

I have nothing more to say. I have nothing more to imagine. The details have no importance, because they can't touch our lives. The unique, irrevocable act is by definition mine.

I didn't want to be taken for a criminal. Or a madman. My most fundamental wish is that my motives not be misunderstood. I didn't intend to do harm. I didn't want to ruin anything. It wasn't my intention to deprive people of a precious object. I only wished to free us from what was regarded as unsurpassable perfection. I saw myself as someone offering a gift, a way out, a provocation.

I opened my window and beheld It, aglow in Its electric orange veil. I was right. It had to come down, whatever the price...

The recording stops abruptly.

Note: Several versions of this text are in circulation. None of them has been confirmed as authentic.

2 WITNESS STATEMENTS RECORDED THE FOLLOWING DAY

He keeps to himself, we don't see him often. He doesn't socialize like everyone else and rarely speaks. And when he does speak, it's only to say what's absolutely indispensable, and always with his eyes down. We don't know his name.

Z.F., 6:30 p.m.

I've been inside his apartment. There was nothing remarkable in there, and there's nothing remarkable about him, either. He never bothers anyone. He always speaks in a very low voice, and quite formally. He's very polite. His little bachelor pad is clean and tidy. I remember that there was a big sofa with a red throw on it and lots of books piled in the corners. He never plays loud music. He has no friends. He gives no trouble.

M.P., 8:18 p.m.

He's a sensitive person with a lively intelligence. Not a very sociable guy, but I'm sure he's very clever. As far as I'm concerned, I'd totally trust him. He seems like he knows how to gauge people.

Ch.S., 8:27 p.m.

I see him every day, charging along in a hurry and then waiting impatiently at the entrance. Every morning. He puts his left hand on the metal and taps out the seconds on the pavement with the tip of his right shoe. He's very conscientious. He arrives at the same time every day and always waits in the same posture. I've frequently felt an urge to follow him. I don't want to speak to him or learn what he's like or what his name is. I'd just like to follow him for a little while, find out where he goes, take the same route he takes. I want to see who he talks to and hear the sound of his voice. I want to see how he moves when he puts his wallet back in his pocket. I want to see how he moves in the midst of all the other visitors. But I've never been in the right mood for doing that. Or maybe, deep inside, I'm afraid to do such a thing. You know, it's enough for me to see him pass. And to imagine where he's going and what he sounds like and how he puts away his wallet.

Z.Ch., 8:37 p.m.

He passed by here last Tuesday. It had been a while since we'd seen him. I've heard he lives alone now. I don't know anything about his family. Just that they never come to visit him. Who knows? He's never talked about them. As if they didn't exist. Maybe it's better that way. We ask no questions. It was around six in the evening when he came by. He's got money. He doesn't need to work. Once he said he'd explain to me about all that, but he didn't keep his promise.

X.O., 8:25 p.m.

I've never heard of whoever it is you're talking about.

    V.D., 9:02 a.m.

He doesn't express himself easily, and often his imagination provokes him to unexpected reactions. Sometimes he'll tell me about extravagant projects, and at other times he'll announce successes that don't correspond to any reality. He writes poetry. In any case, he sees the world with different eyes, and he wants to change many of the things around him. When you get right down to it, isn't that what we all want?

    X.O., 10:45 p.m.

The man you're asking about doesn't exist.

    V.D., 10:10 a.m.

He goes on long walks in the afternoon, all by himself, and it's not easy to guess what's going on in his head. Sometimes he ends up in a movie theater, and sometimes he visits his old haunts, places we've long since stopped going to. He never fails to hike up to the top of the city. He likes looking down on the streets from up there.

    A.T., 2:12 p.m.

I watched him wandering around aimlessly, which made me curious. He made no attempt to hide. Was he waiting for someone, or just idling, wasting time? I couldn't say. He seemed to be hesitating between two possibilities. As if he didn't know what to do. He seemed a bit lost. I didn't consider him suspicious, so I gave him no further thought.

He loitered around for an hour or so and then disappeared. I saw him only that one time, but he made an impression on me.

E.Z., 11:33 a.m.

I don't remember . . .

A.T., 12:58 p.m.

He likes to exaggerate things and turn every decision into a drama. He imagines that he can save the world, or at least that he knows the formula for success in world-saving. He refuses to grow up. He's still a little boy. He's possessed by a conception peculiar to him, namely adolescent messianism. He has ideas and ideals. He likes to dream big. He's heroic. His language is romantic. He speaks in grandiose sentences. He's pretty stubborn.

G.V.M., 1:24 p.m.

Unfortunately, he's a hardheaded kid who refuses to back down. I say "unfortunately" because he hurts the people around him. He's a neurotic. He quarrels with people and things. He comes to blows with inanimate objects, with abstract ideas, words, and phrases. There's something eerie about him. That's also his charm.

Ch.Ch., 3:48 p.m.

He needs to be left alone. People like him can't put up with others very long. People like him need to stay far away from everyone else. He needs to be left alone.

K.F., 8:32 a.m.

He's a complicated and irresolute man. He doesn't know what he wants and changes his opinions instantaneously. He's fickle. Unpredictable. What saves him in the end, I think, is cowardice. He's fearful, he's afraid of everything. He may not seem like the type, but he's often scared by his own imagination, his own thoughts frighten him. His fear makes him timid. His fear makes him use grand words. He puts his intentions into speech and hides behind it. He gets lost in the big things he thinks about. His great expectations give him cover. And so sometimes I have trouble recognizing him.

E.Z., 10:09 a.m.

NEWS

Our Acropolis, our city's summit, has been orphaned. Many people continue to gather at the scene, and there have been numerous manifestations of legitimate anger. The early rumor denying the catastrophe has been definitively laid to rest. We can no longer hide behind the denial of reality that soothed and comforted us during the first days. We can no longer pretend that the disaster didn't occur.

It's difficult: The loftiest emblem of our city is gone, and no one can get used to it. Even the street names sound sarcastic, as though they were there to underscore the loss. In the place where our most representative, our most precious symbol once stood, there is now nothing but empty sky and a pitiful spectacle of destruction and ruin.

The announcement of the definitive version of the events merely exacerbated the general impatience. The final text — a scant few lines written in wooden language — dealt with only the most superficial aspects of the subject. The news was sudden and arrived without any warning. Without any clarification or explanation. It offered us no reassurance. It couldn't persuade us to be consoled. It was a written announcement, but the name of its author was not mentioned. The possibility that questions might be forthcoming was discounted.

On Friday the 17th of the present month, at 8:13 p.m., a small, almost inaudible explosion briefly illuminated, like a spark, the architectural complex that stands on the summit of the city. The site was lit up amid an inexplicable silence. The dazzling white flash even eclipsed the floodlights for a moment. Then all light was suddenly extinguished, and a cloud of dust and smoke enveloped the summit of the hill. After that, the muffled cracking of the collapsing marble could be heard. A little flame cast a faint glow on the city's summit, which for the first time was plunged into darkness.

Shortly afterward came the sound of a second explosion. Dozens of people started running frantically, but they couldn't get through the rubble. Nobody knew what had happened. Nobody could imagine what had happened. The catastrophe had taken place all at once, almost silently, like some wholly unthinkable event that can't be true. A feeling of apathy and perplexity took hold of the city. People couldn't believe their eyes. Passersby looked up in confusion. Shops and offices emptied out, services were suspended. Thousands of people went out into the streets, and there they remained, silent, unmoving, their eyes raised to the summit of the city. Life was paralyzed. Buses and cars came to a stop in the middle of the street; drivers climbed out of their vehicles and stood, transfixed and voiceless, in the roadway, their eyes all turned in the same direction. Nothing was moving. As if time had frozen. An uncanny stillness reigned everywhere. The balconies of the apartment buildings and hotels in the city center were filled with enraptured, destitute spectators. Life had come to a halt. Only a single, slender flame still seemed to be smoldering on the summit of the city. Nothing happened. For hours and hours, we held our breath, powerless to do anything else. For hours and hours, everything stood still.

After night fell, the crowd gradually dispersed, and the numbed city slowly came back to life. A few people found the courage to approach the rock.

Helicopters patrolled above the city all night long, shredding the dark sky with their spotlights. The whole population spent that evening shut up in their homes.

The difficult and disagreeable task of estimating the damage commenced with the first light of day. The spectacle was disheartening. The monument had been literally pulverized. A small crater had opened up in the center of the rock. The structures that remained standing had likewise been transformed into heaps of half-demolished rubble. Blocks of marble and pieces of metal — from the scaffolding used in the restoration work — had been flung in all directions. Unfortunately, a large chunk of rock blasted off by the explosion had damaged the Odeon of Herodes Atticus, the amphitheater on the slope below. The windows of the museum at the foot of the hill had been left intact, and they reflected the now-empty sky.

Qualified experts were summoned and proved unable to conceal their desolation when they announced that the catastrophe was irreversible. Their spokesman could not contain his emotion.

The experts' findings included the first account of the events. According to their calculations, the blast was caused by plastic explosive material, professionally deployed; this latter detail aroused suspicion. The detonating mechanism consisted of a standard horological device with a clock, detonator, batteries, etc.

The perpetrator had closely studied the architecture of the site, and it is conjectured that he had a good knowledge of static mechanics. In fact, he meticulously distributed the proper amounts of explosive material among the joints and seams of the building, including those in the drums of the columns. The monument, weakened by the passage of the centuries, could offer little resistance. Its Pentelic marble skeleton crumbled at once. The first explosion provoked a collapse in the center of the temple. After the edifice had been brought down and reduced to a mountain of ruins, the main cache of explosives, which had been placed in the center, detonated. The cranes and scaffolding then augmented the disaster by falling and crushing whatever the explosion had left standing.

By the following day, a large-scale police operation had already been unleashed. Thousands of suspects were rounded up by the Security Forces. People were afraid, and everyone looked with suspicion on everyone else. The greatest anxiety was caused when one person said of another, "Deep down, he approves of what happened." And indeed, there were some who did approve of it. At the same time, the media sprang into action, investigating a series of potential suspects and searching for the instigators of the crime. Even the metropolitan archbishop was praying for the discovery of the perpetrators, given that — as everyone knows — the ruined architectural masterpiece had during one period of its history served as a Christian church.

Even though human rights organizations accused the police of persecuting immigrants, marginal political groups, and other undesirables, and despite scattered outbreaks of racist violence, the investigation was immediately crowned with success. The perpetrator was traced to the roof terrace of the apartment building in the center of town where he lived. Preparatory sketches for his criminal act were found in his possession. He was an unemployed male named Ch.K. (only his initials were released to the public), twenty-one, clearly an individual of antisocial tendencies. According to currently available information, Ch.K. put into action a plan elaborated over a long period of time and based on detailed on-site inspections. The young man set his deadly charges on Friday afternoon. Afterward, he followed the macabre sequence of events from his hideout. Reports indicate that the suspect's arrest was inevitable, since he himself had shouted in triumph from the roof of his building after the final explosion.

An unexpected silence surrounds the question of the perpetrator's motive. According to unverified information, Ch.K. signed a confession in which he explained what had led him to commit his odious act. The authorities have refused to confirm such conjectures, and they have let it be known that they are dealing with a psychopathological personality. The official announcement states that Ch.K.

could give no rational explanation for what he had done. His action was — in its essence — gratuitous.

Finally, the location and conditions of his confinement remain unknown. No information concerning his future fate has been divulged, and it has not been deemed advisable to publish his photograph.

4 DISCOVERY

The following proclamation, photocopied from the pages of a book, was found during a search of the culprit Ch.K.'s apartment. It is presented here exactly as it appears in the original.

BLOW UP THE ACROPOLIS!
Society of Aesthetic Saboteurs of Antiquities
Proclamation No. 1

Having in common an aesthetic and a worldview that comprehend the destruction and mortality of all forms of being as an integral part of life;

Having set as our goal the destruction of the Parthenon, with as a further goal the rendition thereof to its essential eternity, which is nothing more or less than the standardized flux of unconscious form, including in all likelihood a fecund, spontaneous transmutation of matter, which we erroneously call loss;

Considering that man is doubtless nothing other than an indirect automatism and a natural, resourceful manifestation, and in any case recognizing that a work of art is something fundamentally egregious and foreign to life, and detesting the temporal and historical conservation of such work;

Having understood that the necessity of eternity is one of the fundamental presuppositions of life and therefore of art, since art is but a subversive adaptation of life's fundamental instincts, and moreover understanding that only this necessity is indispensable at the moment of creation;

Acknowledging Salvador Dalí, who had the audacity to compose a work of art made of raw meat and vegetables (no matter whether he mentally intended the work for eternity, for God, or for himself, those words all having the same meaning from the human point of view, although their essence is underappreciated), and therefore acknowledging said artist as equal to Phidias, who did indeed assure his work a permanence through the ages but achieved nothing more within the framework of existentialist eternity, which knows neither number nor duration and for which a second is equivalent to three billion eons, thanks to its volitional qualities and tonal dynamism, which have no meaning except at the atomic level, irrespective of the quantity of the atoms themselves;

Observing that the notion of the conservation of an object through time and history is what is most foreign and illusory for mankind, and furthermore abhorring the National Tourism Organization and the nightmarish journalism apropos thereto;

Convinced that we are preparing a psychically and artistically superior action, and proud thereof in both its aesthetic and its vital dimensions as we institute this form of nihilism, and being certain that a ridiculous and illusory survival cannot be compared, if only because it is inferior, to a single minute of energetic and enjoyable activity, and moreover that said survival is artistically harmful, for it fosters only amateur tourists and eunuchs, along with onanistic contemporary poets and painters, even if — as in the present case — said survival stems from a historical and aesthetic cycle that is not ours,

WE HAVE DETERMINED

1. To fix as our clear objectives the destruction by explosion of ancient monuments and the dissemination of propaganda against antiquities as well as against everything we dislike.

2. To make our first act of destruction and explosion the definitive demolition of the Parthenon, which is literally suffocating us.

[*Items 3 through 9 are missing.*]

10. The goal of this Proclamation is merely to declare the scale of the goals we have set for ourselves. We launch this missile with little chance of reaching most people, but in point of fact, our targets constitute only a small minority.

"Only one is enough." [*handwritten marginal inscription*]

Y.V.M., Secretary-General of SASA

5 RELATIVE TO THE PROCLAMATION OF YORGOS V. MAKRIS

Relative to the proclamation of the poet Yorgos V. Makris (Y.V.M.), which was found in the apartment formerly occupied by the perpetrator Ch.K., said document having been photocopied from a book and annotated in said perpetrator's handwriting, the following witness statements are hereby provided.

WITNESS STATEMENT OF THE WRITER LEONIDAS CHRISTAKIS (1928–2009)[2]

Now and again, in suitable circumstances, Yorgos Makris would make various facetious remarks, which many of his auditors regarded as extremist ideas, and which they took seriously enough to store in their memory. Among the targets of the criticisms he spouted in cafés or at friends' houses in those days was the national obsession with ancestry, which he considered responsible for Greece's intellectual and ideological decline, and — depending on the makeup of his audience — he might end with a recommendation: "Raze the Acropolis!" This idea appeared in print in a Proclamation he published on November 18, 1944.[3] The inspiration for his text, however, came from the surrealist poet Nikitas Randos or Nicolas Calas or M. Spieros — pseudonyms of Niko Kalamaris — who in 1935 had fervently championed this cause in conversations with a circle of friends, before whom he proclaimed (not in a nihilistic spirit but rather with the idea of renovating the philosophical tendencies prevalent in the period between the wars and amplifying the late echoes of Dadaism in Greece): "Let's blow up the Parthenon! Its influence on philosophy is deadly!" It's pointless, in my view, to comment on the laudable intentions of those two poets, as they are no longer of this world, while the Parthenon is still with us. It should be noted here that all this talk about destroying the Acropolis was going on many years before Mao's Cultural Revolution [...] Yorgos Makris was twenty-one years old when he drafted his "Proclamation No. 1." If you consider the fact that Greece had just been freed from the German yoke and take into account the end of World War II and the turmoil provoked in the country by communist ideas, the new — and revolutionary — content of Makris's utopian Proclamation seems to have been not only thoroughly justified but also prophetic. Just think about the phenomenal development of the tourist industry and about what was even then already becoming our ideological poverty in the area of travel and tourism.

Meanwhile, with the December 1944 uprising and its attendant battles between right-wing and communist combatants in and around Athens, and with the battles of the civil war that broke out shortly thereafter, the idea of blowing up the Parthenon mostly faded away. But Makris never stopped talking about it, and it came up regularly in his conversations with his friends — in suitable circumstances — at least until 1960.

LEONIDAS CHRISTAKIS: SECOND STATEMENT

Yorgos Makris was born in Athens in 1923 to extremely strict parents; he was an only child. His father was in the judiciary, and his authoritarian character led him to exercise his profession even within the family circle. At the age of six, Yorgos Makris was injured in a car crash that left him lame and made it difficult for him to walk for the rest of his life. He registered as a student in the law school in Athens but never set foot in the place. He learned French, German, and English and maniacally read all the important writers of the time. From 1948 on, he lived practically alone. He had no particular interests and went from one café to the other, from bar to bar, negligently spending his mother's money and then finding himself broke for weeks. He wasn't very talkative, but he had a great sense of humor. He always had a book or a magazine in his hand, and he'd spend his time reading, sprawled on a chair in a tea salon or café on Kolonaki Square. Sometimes he'd settle down in a café and not leave for twenty-four hours. At other times, he'd stay shut up in his room. He wrote, translated, and maintained a correspondence with friends and acquaintances. His writings showed the influence of postwar existentialist ideas. His poems (he wrote mostly poems) more often than not reflected his psychological or emotional state. His translations were more closely aligned with his philosophical views. He completed three translations: books by Aldous Huxley, Octavio Paz, and Jean [sic] Miró. In 1965, his suicidal tendencies made their first appearance. If we count a few suspect automobile accidents — in the end, his car gave up the ghost — the number of his failed suicide attempts reaches seven. At the end of January 1968, he came to my place in the middle of the day. He looked pale and thin. We had lunch, and afterward he said, "I'm ashamed of being unable to put a decisive end to my life." Then he left. I kept calling and calling him on the phone, but he didn't answer. On January 31, in the evening, someone called up and told me Yorgos had fallen from the roof terrace of his apartment building. Just before, in answer to a question from the doorman, he had said, "I'll be right down."

WITNESS STATEMENT OF YANNIS RIGOPOULOS[4]

[...] But Makris changed all of a sudden. He became mistrustful. He talked about a conspiracy against him. He grew sullen. He neglected himself completely. In 1966, he made two suicide attempts. Then another one in March 1967. He was interned in a psychiatric clinic. In May 1967, he got out, apparently in much better health. But his intellectual clarity was gone, his mind disturbed. He was utterly disorganized. [...] At the end of November, he tried to kill himself again. He was found to be in a state of "structural paranoid delirium with dissociative disorder and persecution complex." He felt that the whole world had it in for him, mistreated him, and believed the unjust charges brought against him. He was interned again, but thanks to an intervention by one of his uncles, he came out of the clinic in December.

WITNESS STATEMENT OF TAKIS MAVROS

In the fall of 1943, he was sent to a German concentration camp in Tripoli, where he remained a long time and barely escaped execution. Every morning, a German would come into the inmates' quarters, and with Yorgos's help he'd call out the prisoner who was slated for execution that day. [...] Years later, a doctor* from Argos who had lost his son to the Germans circulated a notebook in which he'd written down his recollections. In one passage, he made a vague allusion to Makris, characterizing him without any explanation as a traitor. Only because Yorgos spoke German, and the Germans had used him as an interpreter. [...] That baseless accusation haunted Makris incessantly, persistently, and I would say pathologically. All conversations ended with him asking, "Why did they think I was a traitor?" [...] That psychosis pursued him until he died.

WITNESS STATEMENT OF ANGELOS KARAKALOS

I went to see him at his place, 4 Semitelou Street. He was obviously in great mental distress and completely confused. [...] I suggested that he should go to France and consult a doctor I trusted. He said he didn't have a passport. [...] A few days later, at nightfall on January 31, he jumped off the roof terrace of his apartment building, at the corner of Michalakapoulou and Semitelou Streets. He was identified from the passport found in his pocket.

---

* *Author's note*: His name was Boukouras.

LEONIDAS CHRISTAKIS: THIRD STATEMENT

SASA was the Society of Aesthetic Saboteurs of Antiquities, and "Proclamation No. 1" is dated November 18, 1944 (a few days before the beginning of the December 1944 uprising). The initials Y.V.M. stand for Yorgos Vassiliou Makris. Makris included his patronymic so that there could be no doubt that the secretary-general of SASA was himself. The Proclamation was published in 1986, in the only book ever dedicated to Yorgos Makris's work, an anthology entitled *Writings of Yorgos V. Makris* (Estia, 1986), edited by Epaminondas Ch. Gonatas. Unfortunately, the text of the Proclamation appears in truncated form (abridged by the editor?): It's lacking items 3 through 9, which covered the project's organizational aspects. It appears that the edition was censored out of a fear that the editor and publisher of the book could be accused of moral responsibility for any eventual destruction of archaeological treasures and/or historical monuments.

6 A GUARD'S BRIEF STATEMENT

Spontaneously, without hesitating, but with a kind of deferential affectation in his manner of speaking and an artificiality in his tone. As if he were talking about some important person.

What can I say? I'm lost for words. So many years... Every morning, I was the first person to see It. I would always go in right before daybreak, check all the gates, and open the visitors' book. Plenty of visitors would come through every day.

He stops talking and then starts over from the beginning, pompously.

It was summer, the place was overflowing with people. You couldn't distinguish individual faces on the surveillance screens. The crowd was too dense. The cameras scanned an undifferentiated, moving mass of visitors. The heat was insufferable. I stood out in front of the office for a while, finding it very hard to concentrate on my work. My thoughts just kept on straying. The noise was impossible to bear; the visitors' footsteps and conversations produced a continuous, indistinct murmur. There was no rhythm or variation in intensity, just one single, monotonous, appalling note held for hours on end. And people climbing up, interminably, in an endless stream.

By noon of that day, fatigue, the sun, and the excruciating heat had hypnotized us all. Nevertheless, that was the very day when I heard It calling me. Very clearly, through the constant muttering of the crowd, above the voices and the chaos. Surprised as I was, my first reaction was to take my head in my hands and rub my face, as hard as I could. I felt certain my mind was playing tricks on me again. The midday period was always unbearable. I leaned my perspiring shoulders against the corner and closed my eyes. I heard It whispering to me through the wall, like prisoners communicating from cell to cell. It was real, what I heard.

I looked around me. No one had noticed anything at all. I turned my eyes to the surveillance screens. Nothing unusual. The same inexhaustible flood of people. And yet, I continued to sense Its presence.

I went out onto the main path and stopped in the middle of the crowd. Wherever I looked, unfamiliar, indifferent faces were moving past me. And It kept calling to me, more and more distinctly. Without words. As if Its thoughts were capable of calling out to mine. I turned right and left, but I couldn't identify the source of the voice. It seemed it might be coming from the mouth of one of the tourists. From the buildings down in the city. From the streets. Through the tree trunks. The stones or the sun might have been talking. The clouds. It was as if the very air were reciting the same invocation. The whole city was speaking to me.

I closed my eyes and gathered all my strength. I had

to understand how It was communicating with me. Whether intuition, some mysterious magnetism, or who knows what other kind of force was at work; whether It Itself was really what I heard, calling to me from the summit of the city; or whether my imagination was fabricating that nightmare. Then everything stopped at once. As if all sound had suddenly been turned off. Not a living soul could be heard. The visitors seemed to be flowing past without touching the ground. Their heavy breathing slowed, as though a silent puff of air had cooled their faces. They stopped talking. Their clothes undulated gently and languidly, like the fins of fish in the depths of the ocean. Everything had become so crystalline, so limpid. *It* had fallen silent, and Its silence had hushed the whole city. Who knows what had really happened?

And suddenly it was all over. As if reality had gone away for a moment and then returned. The resounding, deafening voices, the tramping feet, the clattering steps, the sleeves rubbing against clothes, the heat, the unendurable sun.

I know now that what It was asking for was my presence, at that precise moment, up there on the rock. Perhaps something unprecedented had been avoided on that very day, or perhaps something abominable had been set in motion at just that moment. And just that time, just that one time, I'm sure It called out to me, and I was unable to respond to It.

He pauses briefly and then resumes, but now he speaks more slowly and in a somewhat more dramatic tone.

What else can I say? I went up the first day after the catastrophe and couldn't believe my eyes. It had been there for so many centuries, you would have thought It had Its own part of the sky. And now, in the place where It had once stood, there was a great expanse of horizon.

I stepped over the iron barrier, which had been destroyed. How had that happened? What words can I use to describe what I saw? Everything around me was black. The ground was muddy, and marble fragments were scattered everywhere. I took the little path that leads to the summit, and at every step I thought my heart was going to stop. No stone was in its place. Everything was topsy-turvy. The ground was covered with a thin film of dust, and little flames were burning among the ruins. The nearer I approached, the more difficult it was to negotiate the path: On every side, all I could see were mutilated pieces of the crumbled structure. It's hard for me to talk about. Everything had collapsed. In the place where It used to stand, all you could see was sky. A sky that appeared to me for the first time in all its breadth, vast and pitiless. Shattered marble everywhere. Intolerable disorder. A wound.

He stops talking, gets up, and takes a few nervous steps, obviously trying to control himself.

Who could have done such a thing? Who could have conceived the idea of harming something so . . . It was . . . I feel like I'm losing my mind. It was . . . sacred. How could anyone even touch It? We're orphans now. What's the city without It? Inconceivable. Wasn't It our place of refuge? Didn't It shelter us in time of need?

Our city was insignificant. She was small and couldn't support It any longer, she was unworthy of It and didn't deserve It, and now that's obvious for all to see, but it's too late. She herself, our city, was what killed It. She took revenge on us. Yes, I really believe that: She took revenge on us. She herself chose the method, and — with great care — she picked out the murderer. The instrument. She called him, just as It had called me. I understand now. What called me wasn't It, it was her, it was the city herself. She was putting me to the test. And she put others to the test that same day, until her choice fell on the one who had the guts to strike at the very summit. I too was part of her plan. She spoke to me that day. She spoke to all of us. And on that day, she found the man who could do her will.

He comes forward and sits on a stool on the far left side of the room.

I watched him. During the last few weeks, he came nearly every day. At first, I didn't pay him any attention. There was nothing particular about him. He was one among so many . . . But then he kept coming back, again and again. At different hours of the day. Irregularly. Sometimes he wouldn't show up at all for a few days. And then on other days, he'd come back two or three times. I didn't see him often. Maybe he came more regularly than I was able to observe. Maybe he came when I wasn't on duty. Or maybe he did his best to avoid me. But he'd always come back in the end. I knew I'd see him again. And little by little, his frequent visits made him stand out from the crowd and become easily recognizable. Because otherwise, there was nothing about him worth remarking. He was a taciturn fellow who always walked with his head down. As if he were hiding in the middle of the crowd. He never looked me straight in the eye. Maybe there were a few times when I wasn't able to distinguish him from the rest of the throng. Who knows? It may be that he came more often. As a rule he went up by the main path, walking at a fast, determined pace. He had his own spot, over in a corner by the barrier, and he'd sit there for hours. Sometimes my shift would end and he wouldn't have budged an inch from his post. He was the persevering type. He would just look, that's all. He'd observe avidly. He always stationed himself in the same place and never climbed all the way to the top; he was content to lean against one of the big orange floodlights that came on in the late afternoon. He always took the same path. He never carried anything at all. Not even a bag. He never took his jacket off. He came alone and spoke to no one.

That's mostly how I remember him. Later he started behaving differently. He'd run up the path. He'd leave his corner by the barrier and walk around the monument, circling It again and again. Pacing feverishly, never stopping. He walked over the entire site, every square inch. At a steady gait, as if measuring distances or time. And he'd observe things closely, attentively.

I'd see him bend over to get a better look at something,

shading his eyes from the sun with his hand. He'd pull out a little notebook and write in it. He was constantly making notes. He'd take a few steps, stop suddenly, and write down a thought or something he'd seen. Then he'd start over. A few steps, and then he'd stop and scribble something else.

On several occasions he came with a girl. They didn't speak. They barely exchanged glances. They'd walk without touching each other, and they often drifted off in different directions. I don't know. Afterward he'd go back to being the circumspect visitor I usually saw. Stooping and silent, he'd return to his post next to the floodlight. After this happened two or three times, I stopped being surprised at what he did. I grew familiar with his behavior. There were days when he'd simply sit down by the barrier and meditate. And there were others when he'd walk around and never stop.

I never once approached him. I don't know the sound of his voice, I never spoke to him, I never knew his name. Our eyes never met. Yet I felt a strange sympathy for him. He was dominated by some secret passion, some obsession. I'm sure he loved It. And even though we never had any sort of conversation, even though he might well have been unaware of my existence and I saw him only from afar, on the surveillance screens, an invisible bond nevertheless united us. I always thought I understood him and never tried to bother him. I didn't want to disturb his moments. I felt obliged to respect such devotion. That was ridiculous, you say? I was so blind? So naïve? Why couldn't I spot the man who would be Its destroyer? I can't believe

7 LIST OF INDIVIDUALS MENTIONED BY THE PERPETRATOR CH.K. DURING THE COURSE OF THE INVESTIGATION

. . .

. . .

. . .

. . .

Yorgos Makris

. . .

. . .

3 EVIDENTIARY MATERIAL

Register No.: . . .

Date: . . .

Dossier No.: . . .

Defendant: . . .

Location when found . . .

Case Description: Yorgos Makris Case

. . .

. . .

. . .

. . .

SASA Proclamation No.1

Topographical sketch of the Acropolis

Map of Athens

. . .

Writings of Yorgos V. Makris, edited by Epaminondas
    Ch. Gonatas (Athens: Estia, 1986)

. . .

. . .

Black-and-white photograph of an unknown male

9 THE PHOTOGRAPH[5]

"...DIAPHANOUS, LIKE JAPANESE RICE PAPER"

"Can I talk to you?"

I didn't recognize the voice on the line right away, but I very quickly realized that something was wrong. "Is that you? What's up?"

"It's real this time...turn on your TV...open your window—"

"Hold on a minute. Calm yourself. What's up?"

I hurried over to the window. The only thing I could make out was a thin line of smoke against the background of the early-evening sky. I clicked the television on and stepped close to the screen.

The images were moving so slowly that time seemed to stand still. I quickly read the subtitles and thought about the hysteria that was going to ensue. I'd never imagined such a thing. It was literally unheard of. I watched, but I couldn't believe my eyes.

Then the images returned to ordinary motion and time flowed normally again, confirming that what had happened was indeed real. Except that the scene reminded me of certain static, flat Asian paintings, like those made by Asian artists who paint two-dimensional landscapes, without perspective. Scale, depth, shadow, and the vanishing point have no importance in their work, while at the same time they intentionally leave areas unpainted, so that these can be read as clouds in the sky, or as water in a pool, or as a river, depending on how the viewer's imagination fills in the empty spaces. But in this instance, the empty space could not be filled in by the imagination. No mental effort sufficed to reconstruct the image. Even though what was missing was something so familiar, so near. Something as clear as a simple geometrical figure.

I couldn't hear the news announcer. Nothing could pierce the silence of that moment. Reality seemed delicate and fragile, diaphanous, like Japanese rice paper.

1 SENTENCE AND PUNISHMENT

Darkness. After several seconds, the video starts. A young man is sitting comfortably in a wrought-iron garden chair. He's outside. Some plants are visible behind him. The image "opens up" to the natural world. He's holding a glass of water. In the beginning, he looks at his interlocutor, who's on the left, off-camera and invisible to the viewer. Medium-close shot, as in televised interviews.

I was a young recruit. I hadn't got used to military life yet. I'd been called up only a few months before, and I was still frightened. Even holding a weapon in my hands was hard to get used to, and my boots made walking difficult, and everything was new to me. Whenever I heard my name, it startled me, and I started scurrying around right and left. I was in a constant state of alert, my nerves stayed on edge, and I'd always wonder if I'd be able to get any sleep at night.

He takes a drink of water.

So here's how it was. Lights-out had just been sounded. I'd fallen on my bed and was trying to keep my eyes closed. I had to get up in the middle of the night for sentry duty.

All around me, the others were talking, some even singing as they came back half naked from the shower room. I tried to lie peacefully on my bed.

Nighttime sentry duty was torture. Not because of the sleep deprivation—that was the least of it. Being on my feet for hours didn't bother me, and I didn't mind the darkness. It was the unbearable quiet, with the light from the floodlights on my feet and my loaded weapon in my hands. I wasn't reconciled to the loaded weapon. I was always afraid of it, and I looked on it with great distrust. When we had rifle practice during basic training, I was so scared I kept my eyes closed. I could never shoot with my eyes open.

The camera zooms out. Long shot.

I lay down that evening, but I couldn't shake the nightmare that had pursued me nonstop since my military service began. It was a strange dream, a dead-end vision that changed shape every time, according to the circumstances. Actually, it wasn't a dream so much as it was mental torment. My imagination condemned me to live through everything twice. Not because it made me recall events that had already taken place but because it put things in my mind that were waiting for me in the future. And since army life was unpleasant and predictable, it wasn't hard to imagine what you knew was going to happen.

That unbearable torture began during my army days, and it hasn't left me since. At first I thought it was just a nervous reaction to the hardships of military service. I didn't want to give those visions any greater extension, and that was why I put up with them and kept quiet, how-ever excruciating and relentless they were. Not even when I was on leave could I escape them. The last dreams of the night, just before awakening, were the first moments of the following day.

Brief pause.

I opened my eyes slowly, ran a blurred glance around the room, and took deep breaths. Then I got up, also slowly, and my naked feet froze when they touched the exposed mosaic of the tiled floor.

Camera moves in for a close-up.

A little later, I woke up for real, and then I lived through the whole thing again, right from the start: I slowly opened my blurry eyes, I gave the room a look, I got up with a sigh, and my feet froze when they touched the floor. Then my dream came to mind, and I realized I was reliving the same awakening. And the whole day went by like that. When I was drinking my coffee, a fleeting vision flashed through my thoughts, images of the outside door opening and the dazzling sunlight blinding my eyes. The dust of the road got into my nostrils, and my cheeks red-dened in the heat of the sun. That was all in my mind. But then, later on that same morning, the outside door opened, the sun blinded me, and the dust from the road really did get up in my nostrils. And that was when I real-ized I was crossing the threshold for the second time.

That's what my life was like. Again and again, I per-formed those little, easily predictable activities of life twice. It isn't that I have some strange, prophetic powers at my disposal, because I am absolutely incapable of predict-ing anything at all. It's just those trivial, all too familiar experiences that torture me. And it's not a little thing, this torture, because it makes it hard to distinguish between what happened in reality and what didn't. Time gets tan-gled up. Nothing is unambiguously present. So even when you're out walking, for example, at a given moment you don't know whether you're climbing the steps of some steep street or whether, at the same moment, you're some-where else, climbing those steps in your dreams. Obvi-ously, you'll know for sure later, and you'll land back in reality, but at that precise moment, you're taking a stroll in the void, suspended in time, full of uncertainty. And then, later, you get lost once again. How can you tell if you're walking for real or if it's your imagination running away with you again? It's not easy to live with a mind that's always playing tricks on you.

The camera returns to the medium-close shot of the open-ing. He takes another sip of water.

So, about that day. I closed my eyes and saw, right in front of me, what was going to happen in the middle of the night. The corporal, half asleep, dragged himself to my bed and shoved me awake. He spoke no word. He pulled my blanket off. I got up, groping around and shivering, took up my rifle, put on my helmet and the rest of my gear, and followed him in silence. We marched through the night. The sky was pitch-dark, and we avoided the flood-lights because they blinded us. We reached the guard-house. I looked the sentry I was relieving right in the eye and took the cartridge clip from his hands. I counted. Ten rounds. We exchanged passwords and places, and the cor-poral gestured with his head. They walked away together, with rapid strides. My eyes got used to the intense light of the floodlights. I walked in a tight circle around the sen-try box, dragging my weapon behind me. The rifle butt ground through the gravel, digging a shallow furrow, a barrier that protected my existence for two solid hours and prevented me from getting too far away, even in thought, from the sentries' guardhouse.

And then my mind began to play tricks again. I was lying in the barracks, marching around the sentry box only in my imagination, when in fact I was waiting for the corporal to wake me up so we could start out.

Suddenly I heard voices that yanked me out of my dream. *Here he comes*, I thought, and I opened my eyes. But it wasn't the corporal, it was a young officer, strid-ing among the beds and rousing the soldiers. "Everybody up! On your feet! Get a move on!" We all got dressed in a great dither, some of us cursing, others stamping their feet spitefully on the tiled floor. The officer persisted in shouting, and the atmosphere grew electric with surprise and discontent. I put on my helmet and my gear, and my gestures reminded me of movements I'd made before, or envisioned before.

We lined up in the corridor. I knew it very well, that

corridor, with its bare lightbulbs and its newly painted yellow walls. A long, empty corridor, where footsteps echoed. The officer slowly inspected us. A cartridge belt left open. A chin strap askew. An unbuttoned jacket. He gave us all a final, hurried once-over and bellowed, "Outside!"

The camera pans. The narrator is now looking right into the lens.

Panic-stricken, we assembled in the courtyard. A truck with its engine running was waiting for us. I hurriedly climbed into the rear of the truck and sat down with my back against the freezing metal. Again I remembered the iron bars pressing against my spine. The roaring engine drowned out the noise of our boots. The exhaust fumes choked off any conversational impulses. Nobody spoke. No one had told us where we were headed. No information had been given us. We looked like frightened animals. The canvas tarp above our heads was tied down tight on the sides, so we couldn't see out. We set off with a jolt. The conjectures began, and the fears. Where were they taking us? Why? I didn't want to listen. I leaned on my rifle barrel and fell asleep.

I took hold of the rope with my right hand and stepped on the footboard. I raised my shoulder and let my rifle slide onto my back. "Go on!" the soldier behind me yelled. I found myself in midair for an instant, and in the next I landed awkwardly on asphalt. Had we really stopped? How many minutes had passed — ten, twenty? Had I really jumped out of the truck, or was this another trick of my imagination? Could I still be asleep, leaning on my weapon? Or was I still marching in a circle around the sentry box? No, that wasn't possible. Who could say for sure? What if I was still in bed, still in the barracks?

Medium-close shot, as in the beginning. He stops talking for a few seconds and rubs his forehead with the palm of his hand. He takes a sip of water.

I followed orders almost unconsciously. I fell into line at once. There were fifteen of us, and we were formed into a column. We stood there in the dark, unmoving. The truck's headlights made our breath visible in the frozen air. No one spoke. How many minutes passed like that? Five? Ten? The officer gave a command, and we began to march automatically, without thinking, which wasn't necessary anyway, since all you had to do was follow the person in front of you. You didn't need to know where you were going. Our boots resounded in cadence on the asphalt. Then everything went very fast, in military style, as we obeyed orders with synchronized movements.

"Halt!"

We stopped.

"Left … turn!"

We formed a straight line, as we'd been trained to do.

The truck backed up and turned, and its headlights shone on a small section of the wall. The darkness was total all around, except for the two small, luminous disks made by the headlight beams. The wall was long, extending into the night as far as our eyes could see. The moon seemed to have gone into hiding on purpose, just at that very time.

The young officer walked the length of our line, stepping briskly and placing a single round in each man's hand. My questioning look got no response. I knew that cold, metallic sensation in my palm. It felt as though the bullet wanted to bite, to chew up the flesh and skin that was holding it.

The officer repeated the same phrase fifteen times: "In the chamber." Load the round into the chamber. I obeyed, numbly, without thinking. On command, the bolts of fourteen other rifles, along with mine, snapped shut, sending each cartridge into its weapon's entrails. Fifteen rounds. All ready for firing. With the gentlest squeeze of the trigger . . .

Everything happened in a moment. Almost automatically. A well-orchestrated sequence of brief movements. And afterward, utter confusion of conscience. Two soldiers abruptly emerged from the darkness, dragging a lamentable young man. They stood him against the part of the wall lit up by the headlights and went away. The driver stepped on the gas, and the engine roared. The headlights shone more intensely. I thought about nothing. Then came a series of commands.

"Release safeties."

I released the safety, feeling the metallic click in my fingers.

"Prepare for firing . . . Aim."

I raised my rifle sight and placed the butt of the weapon against my shoulder. I turned my head and rested my cheek on the metal, cold and damp from the dampness of the night. The officer stepped soundlessly behind us and leaned forward toward each of us, whispering some incomprehensible words over our shoulders. His voice was quavering so much that I couldn't understand him . . . I think he was telling us, "Aim at the heart."

I peered down the barrel of my rifle. The young man looked like a doll, like a puppet. He stood there unmoving, with his hands hanging down and a khaki-colored military pillowcase tied over his eyes.

"Ready!"

I put my finger on the trigger and moved it until it stopped at the firing point. I took a deep breath and held it. I raised my rifle barrel a few millimeters. The center of the crosshairs nibbled at his heart. The same fear, the same trembling. The same uncertainty about what was reality.

I was never reconciled to the loaded weapon. Every time, I closed my eyes tight and fired blind.

"Fire!"

I hesitated for an instant, but I reassured myself: If this were real life, I would lay down my weapon and refuse to obey that command. The next moment, I felt an abrupt jolt in my shoulder. The metal against my cheek was suddenly hot. The powder pricked my nostrils. I knew those sensations. I opened my eyes, and the young man had fallen to the ground in a disorderly heap.

Later I learned that fourteen bullets had struck him in the heart. The fifteenth had penetrated his forehead, just above the left eyebrow.

He drinks the small amount of water remaining in his glass.

Once again I found myself marching around the sentry box, making the same tight circles and dragging my weapon behind me, the rifle butt digging a furrow in the gravel. Had I returned, was I back, or had I never left at all?

I was in anguish, thinking hard about whether I had really fired on that young boy or whether it was just my mind playing tricks on me again, and the night when I would indeed pull the trigger was still waiting for me sometime in the future. I've been tormented by doubt ever since then, it keeps me from sleeping. I'm afraid the young officer will wake us up again some night (for real this time?) and order us to form a squad.

He leans against the back of his chair and remains silent for five seconds. Then he turns his gaze left and right, and for an instant he looks straight into the camera. Darkness.

MORAL

The Parthenon was blown up on Friday, the 17th of the current month, at 8:13 p.m.

Ch.K. was executed on Tuesday, the 21st of the current month, at 12:45 a.m. His death was attributed to an unconsidered initiative on the part of the officers responsible for his detention. An investigation into this matter will be conducted.

The perpetrator's justification for his actions is contained in a text he kept in a secret safe-deposit box. After his execution, the unsealed box was burned to cinders, along with its contents. No official copy of the document was preserved. Since that time, numerous texts have surfaced, each claiming to present Ch.K.'s "authentic" confessions.

Construction of the "New Parthenon" has begun on the site of the one that was lost. It is to be completed within fifteen months.

The profanation of the unprofanable
is the political task of the coming generation.

—Giorgio Agamben, *Profanations*

Notes

1. The poem "We few…" is attributed to Lena Tsou-chlou, who was a member of Yorgos Makris's circle. The Coalition of the Irresponsible, as they were called, was a large group of intellectuals and artists who, beginning in the early 1950s, frequented Kolonaki Square in Athens; they included, among others, Makris, Tsouchlou, Natalia Mela, Takis Vassilakis, and Minos Argyrakis. Tsouchlou's name for them was the Heralds of Chaos. In the collection of Makris's work published by Estia in 1986 (*Writings of Yorgos V. Makris*), "We few…" is credited to "Yorgos Makris's hand, Lena's inspiration." It's not clear whether this attribution was made by Makris himself or by the publication's editor, Epaminondas Ch. Gonatas. Manolis Daloukas makes numerous references to the Coalition of the Irresponsible in a book whose title may be rendered as *Greek Rock: The History of Youth Culture from the Chaos Generation to the Death of Pavlos Sidiropoulos, 1945–1990* (Agyra, 2006).

2. Leonidas Christakis cites Yorgos Makris in a variety of sources, including magazine articles, interviews, and

self-published texts, as well as in his books: *The History of Truth* (Gordios, 2003), *Exarheia Does Not Exist, neither in History, nor on Maps, nor in Life* (Typhlomyga, 2008), *Our Very Own Saints* (Chaos & Koultoura, 1999), and *Yorgos Makris: We Are the Heralds of Chaos* (Chaos & Koultoura, 1992).

3. Presumably, Makris drafted this text the previous day, November 17, 1944.

4. The witness statements made by Makris's friends — Yannis Rigopoulos, Takis Mavros, and Angelos Karakalos — are taken from two symposia (both entitled Yorgos Makris, 1923–1968) conducted in Athens on November 8, 2002, and in Nafplio on November 9, 2002. The excerpts were published in the thirty-two-page booklet *Pioneer* (Nafplio Central Library, 2002).

5. Detail of a photograph in which the writer Kostas Tachtsis appears next to Yorgos Makris.

Acknowledgments

The translator gratefully acknowledges Anne-Laure Brisac's French translation of *The Parthenon Bomber*, published under the title *La Destruction du Parthénon* (Paris: Actes Sud, 2012). Thanks also to Hannah Charlton.

CHRISTOS CHRISSOPOULOS is a novelist, essayist, and translator, and one of the most prolific young prose writers in Greece. He is the author of twelve books, was an Iowa Fellow in 2007, and has won several literary prizes including the Balkanika Prize (2015), the Prix Laure-Bataillon (2014), the Prix Ravachol (2013), and the Academy of Athens Prize (2008). In addition to writing, he is the founder and director of the DaseinFest International Literary Festival in Athens, and since 1999 he has collaborated with the visual artist Diane Neumaier on several art projects and exhibitions.

JOHN CULLEN is the translator of many books from Spanish, French, German, and Italian, including Philippe Claudel's *Brodeck*, Juli Zeh's *Decompression*, Chantal Thomas's *The Exchange of Princesses*, and Kamel Daoud's *The Meursault Investigation*. He lives in upstate New York.

⊞ OTHER PRESS

You might also enjoy these titles from our list:

HOW TO LIVE: A LIFE OF MONTAIGNE
by Sarah Bakewell

WINNER OF THE 2010 NATIONAL BOOK CRITICS
CIRCLE AWARD FOR BIOGRAPHY

A spirited and singular biography of Michel de
Montaigne by way of the questions he posed
and the answers he explored

"A biography in the form of a delightful conversation across the centuries." —*New York Times*

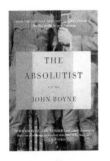

THE ABSOLUTIST by John Boyne

A masterful tale of passion, jealousy, heroism,
and betrayal set in one of the most gruesome
trenches of France during World War I

"A wonderful, sad, tender book that is going to
have an enormous impact on everyone who
reads it." —Colm Tóibín

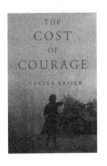

THE COST OF COURAGE by Charles Kaiser

The heroic true story of the three youngest
children of a bourgeois Catholic family who
worked together in the French Resistance

"A thorough and quite accessible history of
Europe's six-year murderous paroxysm...
The Cost of Courage documents, through the
life of an extraordinary family, one of the
20th century's most fascinating events —
the German occupation of the City of Light."
—*Wall Street Journal*

Also recommended:

THE IMPOSSIBLE EXILE: STEFAN ZWEIG AT THE END OF THE WORLD
by George Prochnik

An original study of exile, told through the biography of Austrian writer Stefan Zweig

"Subtle, prodigiously researched, and enduringly human throughout, *The Impossible Exile* is a portrait of a man and of his endless flight."
—*The Economist*

BLOOD BROTHERS by Ernst Haffner

Originally published in 1932 and banned by the Nazis one year later, *Blood Brothers* follows a gang of young boys bound together by unwritten rules and mutual loyalty.

"Haffner's project is journalistic, to portray destitution and criminality without the false sparkle of glamour. His skill in portraiture and the depiction of a social milieu is evident." —*Wall Street Journal*

HIS OWN MAN by Edgard Telles Ribeiro

A Machiavellian tale set during Brazil's dirty war, where the machinations of a consummate diplomat and deceiver ring dangerously true

"Nuanced and psychologically incisive... This tale of international intrigue (Graham Greene might provide the best comparison) shows how malleable concepts of left and right, and right and wrong, can be during extended periods of political unrest and military repression." —*Kirkus Reviews* (starred)